Bedlam

Michaella Erica

Ukiyoto Publishing

Contents

Important Update: 30 Newly Byproducts

Thank you for your consideration, Mr. Sanders.

We selected the ones who are capable of three / or five skills.

Emily Felton's nephew is the perfect candidate for this company to grow

Charlie Felton shall yet be confirmed to be grouped with the first twenty patients (before him), once the doctors successfully removed his memories in the atrium.

But to those who may have not reached our expectations: a patient with three to/ or five skills, and an IQ that ranges ninety and above; shall be put in the laboratory for the ongoing experiments/ exploit them for beta–testing.

Through this cautious act, we already interview nine of the thirty participants who have registered since morning. Hence, they will have to sign on the list of beta-testers no later than 3:00 p.m. Charlie will not be able to remember his relatives and his childhood during and after the experiment, assumingly.

Email sent by, Anthony Miller (Research Specialist). And Richard Desmond (Research Assistant)

Phase I - A Child's Dreams

The Canvas

I'll lose what I've seen in this room, as always.

Fifty-nine children, all clothed in linen, and hair that are shaven.

Thick cushions in fenced beds.

Beds were lined into four divisions, and every end of those divisions has its vinyl record with four men in white jackets—standing beside the recording instruments.

What a usual day.

But I'll lose what I've seen in this room, as always.

Letting the floral elixir wash all over my insides and get absorbed, I put my back flatly on the mattress. Then the weird rhythms come out of the vinyl record—damping my brain with mild exhaustion and making my eyes shut. The doctors said that there is nothing to worry about for the twenty–sixth time, now this is my twenty–seventh day of taking this session. And I still had no clue what do they mean I don't have anything to worry about.

Rhythm per rhythm, I made myself closer to the second surface of my consciousness.

And the presence of the real world that embraces me minutes ago. It dies once I couldn't hear the music anymore. For instance: I am no longer stepping into the room with beds where I came before, I am now standing inside this wide and blank white room, and as I said I am on the second surface of my consciousness. This internal consciousness is my world where I can do anything possible to achieve as I'm asleep. Where all my actions and the scenery I'll establish, will come alive because I am the beholder of my art.

Turning the glossy and cemented material of the walls into less coldly, less solid, less hard, but rough and knitted by a weave. This is the time to put some colors on the white surface I prepared.

My palm tugged out a single stick with silky hair at the tip abound. I handle that single object and begin by creating dots on one of the four walls. Dots are labeled in varieties of hues that my eyes had decided. Even I didn't even think of making a paint substance on a bucket or dyed pastes in containers. I don't need to do it since my eyes have all the colors it collects and distributes out through the brush, much like how a fountain pen works. The only difference was the pen doesn't have any vivid colors, of course.

If the dots of blue, red, purple, yellow, and pink are established from the wall's face. I dare to make a light stroke to separate the colors into half and double the half until all the colors create a luminary effect of a spiral universe. I control the flow of the paint to surround itself the other white walls, now that the family of stars is blooming its radiance and shines more.

The stars that crowded this blank space, are kind of picturesque that must also tap into anyone's soul. To make them realize that their problems are far more uncomplicated than they always know it's unresolvable.

Was there a moment I experienced something that went unwell? What am I truly been through the whole time? Where did I get this idea of talking about problems if I don't see any predicaments happening inside my mind for the past few weeks? So, how come I'm too aware of what things can make me feel good from what is worse if I don't have much memory about myself other than my dreams? How strange this is.

Spreading the colors altogether, now the galaxy is over. No more galaxy this time around.

Painting another world. I made a world of layers of clouds compiled, with powerful angels guarding every place as they are the ornaments for this canvas I made. I gave them their instruments to produce a harmonic rhythm for the wind to sing along and bring light beneath the heaven. Then the darkness will fear them.

I stand below the clouds and raise my brush to capture the light and smudge all of them to strengthen the shine. And as the shine bleeds through the frosted cliffs of the north, the grains from the east, the flowers from the west, and the brooks and river from the south—I have shared the heaven's shine with them to bless their morning.

I flickered the warm colors on those wrinkled twigs and severed fields, for them to uplift their lives and make them become a member of this little dawn ceremony.

I can feel the flowers' wings have opened and dance along with the restful breeze and the sunshine. I can smell the river where the simplicity and purity streams along with it. I can taste the serenity and wisdom that were planted in every forest and young field until they made my soul breathe in harmony.

 I shall, then, give myself a treat for a while. A treat that'll make my eyes feast on the magic and beauty.

From here in this sky, I composed hundreds of doves by dissolving the clouds from one to the other, until the wings, the heads, the tails, the feet, and the eyes are formed.

I command them to spread their wings and told them the rules that I'll be their captain here and there. They never hesitated and showed me a deserving chirp and bow.

We all rise above the tallest cliffs and clouds of white, peach, and gold hues. We dive up, dive down then spin as we fly. We divided into a few groups, crossing every rocky obstacle, boosting our speed, and came back together again as a whole. We haste ourselves to chase the shining light of the sun by breaking the layers of thick horizons. And as we are on the horizon, the sun has now greeted us before the blazing phoenix upon our direction entered the sun's face.

Mystical whales made of cosmic clouds and golden sand have appeared from the blue sky. And I and the groups of avian are coming along with the whales as we finally pass the sun's warm face. Then we grasp the powerful feeling of wonder and the lightness as a feather's weight.

From passing the sun, loaded diamond walls are blocking our path. We break each barrier one by one, and at the last barrier we have ever hit, we perceived another ocean laying below the afternoon sky. And underneath the ocean, an ancient kingdom of gods, and elf houses has bloomed all at once.

The avian formed into winged horses, fiercely armored fairies, and archangels, and one alicorn chooses me to be its rider. The whales remained their same features but they come towards the ocean to swim further into their ancestral habitats. And I have been covered with the clothes of an emperor, an emperor who rides on his horse all over the skyscape with no brakes or limits.

If the night comes by, I will burn the black palette with my flaming colors of the north of soft green, pink, yellow, and blue. Then let them conquer the clouds that soaked in pitch black and crimson. I will splat the hues of the sun, separating them into trillions, and let them fly with their wings before they can infest the grey grass and trees.

I will never let the darkness take everything I crafted. I will save the essence of life and keep them in a jar forevermore.

The Harvest Month

Dry leaves cross the aquatic road where the glint of the sun bleeds through.

Pink cotton candies blush the yellow sky and become a playground for the birds to pass in circles like a moving carousel. And some of them went back to their wrinkling and wooden shelter with dozens of brown bushes sitting on every twig.

I sat down on the violin's cold bench nearby the yellow tree, before the violin's strings produce a chime from the quick touch of a maple leaf. Then my curiosity just sparks, all thanks to the sudden chime.

Turning my paintbrush into a fiddlestick, and exciting the forest to hear just one song, I stood up and play the violin.

Mother Earth's voices are my notes to recreate, it was fast but frail to imitate. Such as the hasting flap of the tree's hair, the unexpected force of the breeze, and the fidgeting fall of the leaves before it lands on the maple foliage.

I crossed ahead the bridge to perceive more details from the other side of the river. The streams that come down from the bamboo sticks, lead my tones to sharpen and go lower then move up, and go down again until it flows smoother. A smooth flow such as how weaker the water goes.

Later on, the birds' chirps interrupted my attention.

To pull up my neutral notes from the birds' song and the curve movements as they fly. I must follow them where they would go and stop by. But as the birds flew faster, and the quicker

I move my feet. My music has to be quicker, either.

And when we all stopped together towards the oak tree—a couple of reindeer, squirrels, beavers, and woodpeckers stood beside the tree and gazed at me. And slowly glances at my instrument when I move down the violin's strings with my fiddlestick.

I resume playing any rhythm I can make and walk away from them. But all of them are coming towards me and dare to hear the song. There was no reason to be scared, so I began to play and let them follow me wherever I go.

Fortifying the forest's spirit with brightness and lively from the moves of my notes. I can assure myself—as I'm elevating the strung of my violin in any direction—all details of Mother Earth's beauty will be convincing and she'll feel the beauty I shared. The beauty and the lightness I craft in this song for her is an offer after giving me her pieces of joy, hope, and inspiration. I thank her for nourishing my soul, *but under what circumstances? Am I already broken? I can't be.*

I shut my eyes as I play, and use the melody to be my pathway.

At first, the warmness of the wind wraps around my shoulders, and the bird's voices can be heard above my ears. I remain myself to be steady and practical when imitating Mother Earth's voice.

But as I sped up the notes through what I heard from somewhere else, a loosened string slap the back of my palm at the moment the clouds gurgled and yawped.

I lose my melody. I lose my path.

I'm standing in this meadow of drought, decay, grey, and unloved. And the animals seem to have disappeared on my guard.

The Village

Where am I?

The dawn is dead and cold but not as cold as the biting winter. The grasses haven't been fed with the clouds' tears, and even so, the breath of the sky was washed in grey and mute like a ghost that lurks elsewhere. There are no birds that can become the sky's performers. But there is only the never–ending soulless sky, with the never–ending gray of hairy ground to gaze at. And the never–ending dawn with no sunshine can come out of the grumpy clouds.

Further beside me, an oasis of bricked, dirty, and gothic shelters and parishes are standing to one another like a maze. So, looking away from the wrathful clouds, I decided to discover the gloomed oasis rather than risk my courage to walk beyond where the clouds came to rest.

I raised my instrument and pressed the last strings I have. But as the wind comes to me and fade my only small weapon into ash, it made me behave like a cat on hot bricks. What can I do now? Should I endure all these dead tones that are painted in the village? I didn't create this uncanny world, and I don't think I am going to feel any better if I stay here. I'm starting to think about how my mind created this even if it does not belong in my intentions to build such a place as this.

Do I have a memory? I must walk, I am walking, and I am staring at every building where no lights are coming from the window. My shoulders have been slammed by the crisp air—I can't have anything to warm myself other than rubbing both of my arms with my hands. I kept on walking in a straight direction and I sensed that this place is preventing me to go anywhere by shackling my soul with fearsome and dread.

How can I change this devastating place without my instrument? I don't have anything fantastical and bright inside my imagination, all there was empty! I'm preoccupied, I'm now focused on what my feelings are trying to say more than what my mind is trying to do. I don't know where I should go next.

No birds? No songs? No sun? No moon? No stars? No colors? Where are you all? I can't believe you all disappeared.

Who's behind this dumping me into this horrible land? I'm tired of seeing this lost and aged village! I'm tired of feeling this invisible creature crushing my hope to smile! Why are my eyes leaking some woeful water? Why I can't stop my flinching whispers from crossing out of my lips? Why I sensed that I'm looking for something or people I do not know? Why do I feel like somebody has existed in my life but I'm not sure if they're real? I can't walk for a bit longer.

I couldn't do it. I have to shell myself to respond to this agony, for a while. I do not know who I am. I do not know why I'm here for. Whom am I looking for? Who could they be? I do not

know their names! I do not know what I am to them.

Where are they? I missed them! I missed them very much, but at what circumstances? I have to go away from this land and find my way back to where I'm safe. But I just can't stop myself from resisting this pain! I'm trapped! Help me.

Down Below the Unconscious

Sweet hums of a mother stream through the air and fog my ears.

It pulls me to its chain rhythm, and once I open my eyes and untack myself from my agonizing shell. The world brought me to a room where the red chairs are placed in rows, where the curtains are folded, and where a single light popped from the dark and revealed a plum fairy posing in grace. She dances just the moment, and the instruments below her played by themselves. And I felt the room shaken as the audience appeared on the velvety chairs in out of the blue, and they applauded at the same time.

A spare seat is reserved for me at the front then I do what the others look like and do things as they do.

I sat, and clap, and watch the fairy dance around the porcelain floor. She moves gracefully. Gracefully. She made our heads wave. She made us follow her steps through our eyes, but a drop of red from above cut my senses to stop my imitated actions. Till more drops splat by two, then six, then ten, then more and more than I can count.

No one was interrupted by the drops; everybody is still clapping even though they don't have faces. I look at the fairy, she became a fleshed mountain and doesn't dance. The instruments are fighting because none of them can be the leader to track down the notations properly.

Their notes are blended of a burning disk, a hard strum of a whip, a hum that runs and pauses and leaps whatever it takes, a sum of trumpets is being cursed that imitates the sound of a falling plane, an ambush resounds at the back and a ballad crossing beyond them and out of nowhere.

An unforgivable hymn praying in the room caused my head to swirl like anguish clouds, till I produce heavy rains and multiple claps of thunder I couldn't control to stop. More whirling tunes of an explosion, thud, whip, chant, hit, scratch, shriek, slap, hiss, crack and clap. And ear–bleeding voices of horns that resound the march of executioners and soldiers. Before the black and grey bugs swallowed the chaotic noise with their high–pitched buzz and glitch.

Then stopped.

I've seen myself as a human, again.

No bloody rain is soaking in this room, and the crowd paid more attention to the performance than making applause constantly. The plum fairy takes her final bow as the music resounds its formal and neat execution. The curtains were about to close, not until a fire burst behind the fairy and the walls. Everyone melted while still keeping their smiles, and uplifting their empty eyes as they gaze at me. Nothing seems to be fine.

The hot smell had alerted my beastly nature and craving for freedom as possible. I ran towards the door, gets out, and found another door. I ran and ran as I could, but the floors just pulled to more inches. Then there are shadows are coming towards me, they touch my arms, they release their threads, and they saw my eyes raining. They released their needles, they planted my feet on the floor, they touch my blue lips, and they sew it—it turned red and happy.

I am not happy. I am dying from this hallucinatory fear and infliction continuously.

I failed to reach the door, I was sunk in the shadowy puddle, I was brought back to the white room, I saw my canvas of where the ocean is shown owned a depressing sky, millions of dirty skulls nearby the blood–soaked water, and numbers of gravestones.

I saw my canvas glitch like television and change its subject to be a painting of a summer garden, rivers of spring, and a frosted mountain. It glitches again, now they are nothing but a burning place where the wretched and angry alienated men suffocating from their tormented minds and broken souls.

I saw my canvas change into an artwork of a harvested forest and quickly turn into a mixed portrait of dead animals with their bodies manifested with bugs and flowers, and scrapped organs.

I saw that the painting was added with more heavy brushstrokes. I saw the brushstrokes were carried out by a boy's bleeding paintbrush. I saw his tears flooding through his eyes and making the room flooded by his tears. I saw his hidden scars exposing on his skin. I saw his smiling face stretching down like melting clay. I saw myself.

He's facing me and asked why he can't see the differences between things that are real from what are fake. I do not know the answer. There's nothing real anymore from the dream I invented.

I thought I could create my reality in this unconscious place. But the nightmare that caused everything to change because of its delusionary effect—I don't know if I'm real or not, I don't know who I could be, I do not know anything.

I only said to the boy what my name was, that is the only thing I know. I'm Charlie.

Phase II - Not a Dream as Before
Welcome Back to Reality

Dead Voices

"Charlie. Charlie, wake up."

"Who said that? Who are you? I can't see you in this padded cell."

"We're in here for a very long time. Hundreds of us here in this lunatic chamber died in the material of what we are against. We're done trading our painful whispers, peeling our flesh, hearing the smoke's command to hurt ourselves and decay into the soil from blood and flesh. We bloomed into innocent poppies, tulips, and orchids. But it doesn't mean our freedom has bloomed within it. But we cannot harm you, however, people with white jackets and carrying needles and masks would do any harm, but you can't defend yourself. We did what we must do as much as we believe we can save our lives, but in the end, it was just a failure."

"What life am I living? Why is there so much suffering I have to endure? When could this be over?"

"It's not in your hands to change what path has been given to you, Charlie."

"But this isn't what I deserved. I'm confused and lost."

"So, as we, we never deserve any of this. No one could save us from this mad little world even if you dare to pray for hope."

"I don't know who I am. I don't know what it's like to be a child who thinks nothing but wonder and adventure. I can't remember what my life looked like before I got here in this place."

"All of us are not being treated well like how children should be treated. Rather we are just an advantage for this company to raise a fortune, and blindfolded by the doctors that we'll be healed from our untouchable sickness. But the truth is, they left us tortured and suffering to death. They don't matter about healing us. They just deceived us from the hypnotic air we take, the endless harmony we hear, and the fresh or dull petals we devour are said to be therapeutic for us. But it's an addicting material we're controlled to use for the sake of their demands. This isn't the place for being redeemed as you think. So, there is no such thing as the need to escape from this place. But being stuck in here forever and keep enduring the pain you can't expect next. We're sorry, Charlie."

"If I stopped keeping the next torment I will resist, I can become like you. I am scared and so tired of thinking about this. I just want to go and find my home, but I don't have any tracks left to choose from. I can't take this horrible sadness and the fear of losing more time to hold. I feel like I am almost at my end as the days keep passing by. I just want peace, but who do I have the most to ask for their courage and light? I have never been loved by anyone. I have never been called by someone in a concerned and wholehearted way. No one has ever heard our help from our undescribed pain over and over. Who's going to be there for me when I'm dying? Is this where the meaning of life belongs? Is this where the meaning of life was created?"

"Someone's coming. He's here!"

"Who?"

"Charlie? Where are you?"

"Don't engage with him, Charlie! Just don't!"

"Dear voices, what should I do?"

Phase III - The Diary

Entry No. 1

May 15, 1986—Thursday—8 p.m.

Emily Felton. Deceased.

I found fewer of her documents from the administration office last night. It was not illegal to read someone's paper if they are already deceased like her. Which, the staff would do nothing with her files any longer but dumped them into the reserved box of slush piles.

Emily Felton bought her nephew to this facility to receive treatment for his PTSD and depression. I've also found her written and *cut* record (that was distributed to my father to read before he began giving schedules) of her oral interview that specifies her nephew's profile:

"Good afternoon, and thank you for coming here today. I'm Mister Miller. And what's your name?"

"Emily Felton."

"Can we begin Missis Felton with the interview?"

"Sure."

"Tell me the name of the patient, his IQ, and his age."

"His name is Charlie Felton. He is eleven years old, and his IQ is one hundred five."

"Charlie. Eleven. One. Zero. Five. Okay. Can you tell me what his mother's maiden name was?"

"Anne Fischer."

"Father?"

"Christian Felton."

"Tell me their occupations, and where they work."

"They are both working in the same place. Anne was a theatre singer and a performer, while her husband was a composer."

"Tell me what their relationship was with their son."

"They were good parents. They know how to keep their son's childhood the happiest. They provide his education and gave him proper care and attention. Charlie was also taught how to paint, write, and dance by his mother. While my brother, Christopher Felton, taught Charlie how to play the violin, harp, and piano."

"How did his depression and PTSD occur?"

"After the fire incident in the theatre. Long before that happen, his parents saved a reservation for him as a birthday present last year. Anne had also saved me a seat next to her son so that I can look after him while the play gets rolling. We were all happy. But not until we've seen the fire bursting out from backstage. We've seen how people have died in the fire, but we have never seen Anne and Christian at the time the audiences were evacuating throughout the theatre. I brought Charlie out of the building and noticed him frightened and muted. I know he was looking for his parents, but there were no more guests crossing off the exit once we left. I knew they could never escape."

"After that, you decided to bring him to your home."

"I have sole custody of their son. Charlie is broken. I just wished to see my boy okay and happy. I missed his smiles, but I can't see it once and for all without his parents beside him."

"We're sorry for your loss, Missis Felton."

"That's all right."

"In any case, we are so lucky that you bring Charlie here to this medical center to get him fixed. I will go to the Head Office to get your nephew's therapy schedule later on."

"Can I be with Charlie during his therapy?"

"I'm sorry, Missis Felton. But that was against our will."

"Will? Why not?"

"We would rather suggest you can come back here once Charlie is perfectly complete and healed. And don't worry I will contact you on the phone if there are some good changes to the progress of his state and the therapy."

"Would you suggest any prescription for Charlie to take? Or call one doctor to do the session at home instead of here? Charlie would need me, and he couldn't look after himself."

"Missis Felton, we can assure you. He is going to be okay from here to the end of the day. Turn off the record, Sir Desmond."

Unfortunately, Missis Felton was shot in the forehead after she was caught in the atrium (where visitors are highly prohibited to go inside). She may have seen the process and secrets that she would expose to the public, but father prevented it to happen—by aiming a bullet into Emily's head just to secure the company's reputation and its plans.

Emily failed to save her nephew and uncover the company's illegal business right in front of their false advertisement.

Her risky intentions are mentioned in one of my father's journals, but I haven't learned everything about what the process looks like in real life.

Though, I'm confused, how did she find that advertisement even if this company is so anonymous and unlicensed?

Emily's dead body was thrown into the basement, with other guardians who were killed before her—due to their intention of taking their children away from the doctor's hands.

But for those guardians who weren't killed, this happens from their decision of neglecting their children inside the hospital, with or without a pledge of receiving drugs from the company in exchange.

I think those parents (who pledged) might be unskilled artists, and dare to buy those drugs (that were suggested or promoted to them) by trading their sons and daughters to the doctors, like money. Which, they care more about fulfilling their careers rather than their children's future and security.

So, why did they even create a family life if they are aware of, they can't spare their time and responsibility from their careers to foster one child or some? They should've been unmarried or childless in the first place.

Entry No. 2
July 09, 1986—Wednesday—3 p.m.

I met a nine–year–old patient (Olivia) who is being beta–tested five times and wasn't afraid to share with me her experience inside this place. She tells me first about her schedule that every morning she has to come to the garden to harvest the new plants and pick the grown ones to be used for experimentation and other sessions. Then in the afternoon, she has to help the staff with their task in the atrium before she can take her brunch in the cafeteria for thirty minutes. After thirty minutes, she then goes to the laboratory for her beta–test session.

It was ordinary to hear how she functions around the hospital. However, it was more sinister than I thought. So, she elaborates on every fact I needed to understand.

First of all, the flowers (a.k.a., Mallory flowers): These are used for decreasing the patient's psychological stress, and self–destructive behaviors, and to treat many different conditions. Adult flowers had to be processed on the underground level of the company to turn them into a gas (they are inhalants), and liquid substances (they are injectable or for consumption).

More likely, these flowers are similar to psychotropic drugs and psychoactive drugs in between.

And the types of drugs the staff would prescribe are depending on the individual and their specific symptoms and condition. Patients needed to take their prescribed drugs before and after completing the music session.

Second, the music session (inside the atrium): This is the session that disguises itself as a therapeutic instrument. Most patients with above ninety percent of IQ are placed in bed with a hanging tube that is facing down on their heads. The session would only start after they consumed the liquefied flower in a cup. Once it was done, the staff would play vintage music by using four vinyl record players and timing the session in its specific hour.

As the music continues to play, the patients would fall asleep and float on their beds, until smoke began to steam out of their foreheads.

Olivia compares the smoke's features just the same as the features of a galactic cloud.

She replied, "The patients, look like they are floating in space, in other words."

When the smoke comes out, the tube would absorb all of it while the patients are unconscious in their sleep. The session runs for four hours, and after that, the patients can return to the public dorm room to take their inhalants once more.

Third: The harmful effect of the music session and the Mallory flowers. Patients have to keep participating in the atrium for thirty days in four hours. Some of them were recorded about their creative energy changing its color into darker tones as a sign of having hallucinatory nightmares that originated from their mental illnesses. While others were removed from the public dorm room and prisoned in the padded cell through their self–destructive behavior.

Patients in the padded cell are some of those who have experienced worst episodes than those who were new–listed from the registration form. This happens when they get overdosed on the flowers. Neither the flowers can't keep them away from their self–destructive tendencies. Heart attack due to hallucinations. Brain tumors or any other brain disorders due to creative energy loss. Or memory recovery as a factor.

Which, there's only fifteen percent of them can complete the thirty days period, while the rest take their own lives in the padded cell, or are executed by drug suffocation immediately.

Fourth: the surgery. This was performed in the second section of the atrium, where candidate patients and beta–test patients needed to have their memories removed. This is the first stage before the candidate patients can start with their music session, while the beta–test patients can begin their test session in the laboratory.

Olivia knows the truth. She is, but a byproduct, other than being neglected by her grandparents. She expected herself to be transferred to the padded cell sooner, just like the ones who were after her. She thought that being a beta–tester is different and isn't harmful, but in the end, there's nowhere else for her to find hope and proceed with life.

Entry No. 3

July 13, 1986—Sunday—10 p.m.

I couldn't sleep with all the noises the patients make in the middle of the night. So, I decided to read some of my father's hidden journals from his office without getting caught.

I finished the whole book in half an hour, and I would love the opportunity to recall what I've learned from it by writing here in this entry.

Within his journals, there are hundreds of pictures of patients stamped every single week. And every picture has a printed document pinned in it with silly signatures and blue thumbprints below.

I've seen what these artists were like (the patients) before they were formed to be mad other than becoming the company's sick clients.

I've seen them as poor, rich, traded for money, help seekers, victims of neglect, and psychological punching bags.

I could still remember the beauty, the form, the colors, and the movements that their mind can represent when they were sleeping from the music. It was said in father's journal too, where he describes their dream as a garden where the uncanniness and mix of confusions are blooming itself and throughout the dreamer's head. In short, it was nothing but a dream that people can't fully remember how long it exists and what its entire meaning was once the morning comes.

However, father is missing the point. In my perspective, a dream is a place for containing their happiness, desires, and total comfort; it's an accessible place where they can be able to create anything that they want to do without rules. Perhaps, they can even channel their genius into the dream whenever they are inventing their dreams anytime. For example, a writer can be a character in his book, a musician can play her instruments with the angels, a painter can paint a physical world just by doing different forces of brush strokes, etc.

This is close to saying, that dreams are playing a part as an alternative world where the dreamers can live there and do marvelous things much easier that are impossible to achieve in the real world.

Moreover, most of the patients' dreams are starting from joyous beginnings where they are in their comfortable state and extreme paradise (as how relieving it is for me to feel when I'm staring at their vivid smoke a long time ago). But not until they were pulled down from the darkest level of their creative minds that led, they feel hopeless, paralyzed by their fears, and get lost in their unaddressed illnesses. Their genius was so bright and could be childlike as well. But was constantly squeezed out by *his* apathetic nature, as much as his company's goal caused their bright genius into a nightmarish land.

The patients did not deserve the changes in their minds, but they are more terrified of what they shouldn't become. They didn't deserve to be mad, and even if they are not the reason why they becoming mad, they are being sculpted to the belief that my father has warned me:

"Pain is part of the human condition. So, being tortured is also included in the artist's nature due to romanticizing pain to make themselves greater and appreciated. Neither, some of them can't stop channeling their emotions into everything they create, no matter if it doubles their condition terribly, because that is what they were made to be or what they naturally do. And they don't care what their inner self is saying. They just have to do the job before planning how to make the noose fits in their throat."

He also added, "Look, none of the tortured artists, like them, were rescued in the past centuries. Sylvia Plath, Vincent van Gogh, Edgar Allan Poe, and Robert Schumann; all of them end their lives intentionally. And why should I be bothered to rescue the patients' lives from their sicknesses whether it's caused by their environment? Neither, if it's through biological, physical, social, or no matter the cause; when society destined them to be tortured? Let's be specific, people like me don't matter about what these lunatic and broken artists are been through. Because all of us are built to have different problems that we should only be dealing with. So, it's not my job or yours to help these poor souls deal with their troubles—just let them do that risk themselves if you don't want to have more disturbances to get away from."

No! That is a dangerous allure, and their illnesses don't define them! They did not romanticize pain! They are trying to stay on the positive side of human nature because they are tired of the sufferings that bottled them ever since they were raised in their homes. Ever since they were abused. And ever since they were lonely and broken.

They are not blind or ignorant to be educated that every good life has amounts of distress and sufferings within it.

And they are not fools to take their own lives at risk or let death takes it, just because life is horrible. Instead, they have to be stable as possible by using their passions and gifts only to cope with everything they've been through.

I must save them.

But father is a brute.

Entry No. 4

August 17, 1986—Sunday—noon.

My notions of the candidate patients.

The patients' dreams and their genius, including the galactic smoke from their heads are all intertwined with their creative energy.

It is known that Mallory flowers are used as a distraction for these patients to get away from their psychological stress and self–destructive behaviors. But one thing no one wasn't allowed to tell (according to the company's regulation), is the flowers can act as a booster for stimulating the patient's creative energy up to ninety-nine percent. This means that the more creative energy has boosted, the more chances the patients can get good dreams to produce a higher sum of smoke.

In that case, there would be more drugs the company can manufacture per month.

However, the flowers' stimulant strength can only last twenty-seven to thirty days before it disintegrates. And if that happens, the patient's stress would return and leading them to have several nightmares. Thus, the galactic smoke that is being released will form its tone into a darker shade of grey, red, and blue. It's also a sign that there's not enough creative energy left from the patient. The only thing the flowers can't do is regain or create another creative energy.

In other words, the staff is abusing the patients' creative energy by giving them liquefied mallories twice a day just to make more money as possible, due to the limited days for the flowers to be utilized. So how many times do they have to toxify the patient's health with those flowers? fifty times? sixty times? I can't even imagine how high the patients could be by consuming those drugs sixty times.

Aside from that, if I include the patient's number of hours or days of taking the inhalants after every music session.

Then that would make them blitzed more than sixty or fifty times.

So, leaving the patients addicted or toxifying them is the way for these staff to be paid. How afraid should I be? Or should I be concerned? They are using the patients excessively to earn money as a necessity since the outbreak has left the economy depressed! But suffering the patients every day is not a moral act I can't validate. I can't forgive them. And I wouldn't trust that they will use their money for something valuable for their families. Perhaps, they will use it under worse circumstances.

The nightmare smoke or the dark galactic smoke is what the staff is preventing in the manufacturing process of their product. Just for the sake of the consumer's psychological well–being won't be affected by the patient's mental illnesses.

The life cycle of the flowers and the patient's energy cycle is very similar to how manic–depressive disorder and depressive disorder circulate at each other, doesn't it? I hope so.

The session of taking the patient's memory is a weapon to protect the company's illegal intention away from the government. If the memories weren't removed, these patients would do anything to expose the whole filthy truth about the company by then.

What are the inhalants for once they have completed the music session? What are the staff going to do with those patients who successfully reached the thirty days period? Are the flowers being traded from any stock markets, or is it just belong to the company's experiments too? Where do the flowers come from? Are the flowers has been a strategy to compete with other drug companies that my father is opposed to? I wish I can get his agenda from his private documents.

Entry No. 5
August 27, 1986—Wednesday—9 p.m.

Charlie was in the padded cell; I wish he could remember me. He was a child filled with fantasies and magic in his sleeping mind. His childlike palace helps him to keep his innermost thoughts of hope and happiness. But on this night, he was not the innocent friend I know. He refused to comply with his session due to his impulsive behavior and attempted to finish one nurse's life with a scalpel. But the staff held him out of the atrium quickly as possible and locked him into the padded cell. I never saw what he did in the atrium, but I heard enough rumors from doctors tackling that incident outside of my room.

Charlie wasn't himself. I missed him.

Entry No. 6

August 28, 1986—Thursday—1 p.m.

I spent my break hour looking at Olivia's paintings in her dorm room. Her paintings have all the same features of gardens, sea lakes, and meadows that perfectly exiled the style of an impressionist painter in just a few days.

However, I don't believe all of this work wasn't belongs to her intelligence since she's just a beta–tester. No beta–tester can exile these firm painting techniques when it is possible to admit that she was forced to use any experimented drugs that her scientist will distribute. The drugs made her a genius, not to mention, giving her an alternative intelligence, she doesn't have.

If the drugs nor the experiments had a successful result by turning these beta-testers into incredible artists. Then the consumer would be incredible as well. But they have no clue what's behind the addicting product they consume.

I wonder what Octavia is doing this afternoon. She has to be back in this room where we can talk to each other. I need her here just to make myself feel all right.

Entry No. 7
August 29, 1986—Friday—5 a.m.

Henry. Evalyn. Jacob. Sam. Lucy.

Why are you there in my dreams? It happened again. Why does this have to happen again. What can I do? What should I say?

I'm sorry. I should have saved you.

I should have given my time with you much longer.

I should have saved you, but I don't know how. Forgive me. Forgive me. Forgive me. Forgive me. But I want you to know that I'm trapped too. I just wanted to rest. I couldn't take this flinching memory of your disappearances.

So, please consider that I can also get weak too. I understand why you were there showing your presence when I'm asleep. You are all upset at me because I failed to protect you. We did try, my plan could save you. But it was just an error. A very big disappointment. Until they suffocated you, before father suffered me with his bruising words and the flaming sting of his dressage whip.

Henry. Evalyn. Jacob. Sam. Lucy. I have shed many tears, so please, your friend is already tired. She wanted to sleep. The patches of guilt and sorrow began to killing her soul, but only a little serenity you'll share would do to shut the pain. Please, no more rage. No more rage. No more rage, it is all I beg for.

Entry No. 8

August 29, 1986—Friday—8 a.m.

Condolence for me.

May you rest in peace. My dearest friend, Olivia.

Entry No. 9

August 30, 1986—Saturday—11 a.m.

I wore Olivia's clothes, and it made my buoyancy break apart. Her number become my number and I was signed and already designed to be a material for the laboratory. There's no going back for me anyway to feel safe and sound like in the first place. But be trapped in this frightening process that killed her.

Father beta–tested me and stated that I should have been more useful to him since the day he was raising me. He never waited for me to contribute something myself, so he had to go after his narcissistic expectation by dragging me to his experiments and showing me his ideas of how to be a useful child to her parents.

Doesn't it sound so judgmental and unfair at the same time, that he only sees me like I'm nothing to him? He didn't even cure my anxiety and loneliness after I encountered the deaths of so many people, I cared about the most. I'm so sick of seeing their names sculpted in stones or written in tags. I'm so sick of the remorse and guilt I felt of their demise, and their unexpected disappearances I never wish to happen.

But it just keeps happening, like what it has done to Olivia. It scares me because I feel like it's my turn to be disappeared sooner, and I'll never have the opportunity to reshape my life if that occurs. This is not supposed to be normal to feel; my mother said that to me when we're talking about grief and death. But how would I be braved facing it if he wasn't acting like a good man? A good father? He doesn't know how to be like one.

To sum it all up, he failed me. And with all the suffering I have to resist as the other children do was nothing for him to contemplate.

He, instead, grab me to work on his dirty work and neglected the sense of being a father. He never loved me, and he won't give me a spare room in his mind to help me get out of my problems! I don't feel that I have a father who'll be there for me whenever I need help.

I don't feel the sense of security and attention any longer than in the past when she was there for me all the time. Father hasn't changed even if she's with us, which he couldn't even at least try to be soft and caring to the both of us. What a terrible husband he is. What a terrible man he is to be married to a disciplined and generous woman. What a big contrast to observe.

I'm not his daughter. I wanted to be like one, however, how can I if he just treated me like nothing, or a byproduct, perhaps a lab-rat? This place isn't truly where I belong. I shouldn't be here. I have to go home but mother isn't here. She's my true home and not father who has a different definition of home and fatherhood.

Entry No. 10
September 15, 1986—Monday—1 p.m.

He made me be the worst of myself.

I had no self–control because of the drugs that affected me. I had harmed others and I harmed myself the second time during my session. I don't know what to do to stop that abusive behavior just after I took one of the patient's lives in danger. But that's not who I am and I would never want to hurt anyone. I never do.

I've been insisted to take whatever drugs I'd been given in each hour after hours until I felt like my body is getting poisoned and controlled. I can't take another liquid to consume or smoke to inhale, because my body and my mind are not prepared to get used to the effects. The fact that I did feel the euphoric side effect and the extreme stimulation of my creativity after taking those drugs. I did heavily suffer from various headaches, hallucinations, distortion of memory, and physical harm I do to myself.

It's hard to stop my darker side and being dependent on those euphoric drugs at once. But it's harder to be back on myself and sustain the things that are healthier and better for me.

I'm all aware that drugs aren't specifically the key to removing my troubles since all I need is a person who'll be there for me to restore my courage and get fixed.

Father, you cruel man. You selfish madman! The psychotic air, the flowers, the patients that floats, the deathless grief, the unresolvable pain! These details form themselves like a motion photograph that breaks the pieces of my mask day by day! We never deserve your twisted philosophy that caused us to be tortured.

You have ruined your daughter's life. But you will fear me someday for I am not done with my retribution. I will sculpt you more from what hurts you the most.

This is the end of the entry. My name is Cheryl Sanders. I'm only fourteen years old.

Phase IV - Purgatory

The Deal

"This place. Is this another dream?"

"This isn't a dream, unfortunately. You are stepping into this ground where the existence of mortals has ended, little one. And where you can find the amount of infliction screaming from the cracked mouth of the inferno. As well as the miracle hymn that echoes above the shining sky. This is where your second life belongs. This is where the purified and humble souls are welcomed from the Lord's home, while the ones who cannot be forgiven are tortured forevermore without redemption. Charlie, hold my hand, and I'll take you to your eternal home. Your mother, your father, and your auntie are waiting for you in heaven. But you must vow to rest your dreams to remain in simplicity and peace."

"Wait, I want to know how I died."

"A massive bomb attack happened a few hours ago. It destroyed the entire experiment and none of the people survived in the laboratory after the incident, including you. Nonetheless, the entire filthy work these brute scientists have worked on—finally has been put to an end, where also the harm they manifest won't happen again to any children of the next decades. Mister Sanders has perished with the rest of his crew. His daughter has her agony washed off her to start a new beginning. And you have to be sent away from this purgatory. So, take my hand and you'll see your—"

"Not this time, this can't be the end. I mustn't end. Please, help me get back to the living world and let me live life the way I want to. I have to do my plans."

"Plans? What's the matter, Charlie?"

"I can't just die and surrender the wishes and hopes I had promised myself. I have to use my flair. Not leaving them behind to be wasted. Forgive me, Death. If I'm bothering you by hearing my complaints instead of taking me up there since I came here. I'm not comfortable with this."

"No need to apologize, little one. You're just a young boy, and I know, you're confused, scared, and feeling pity. You have lots of plans that must have been completed. And if only you're still alive surely you can create a legacy out of your numbers of potential. You are a brilliant human being with a brilliant mind. But why are you the only one who refuses death more than those brilliant children I've encountered, who vowed to surrender their dreams to live in heavenly paradise? You're quite a peculiar one. But, now that we're here in this scenario. What shall I offer you? I must address this sudden circumstance for the two of us. What would it be?"

"Death, do you think I can be back alive?"

"However, do you dream of seeing your family up there and being back with them together?"

"I missed them. I—no, I'm not ready to stay with them yet."

"Fair enough, and without any fuss, I may have a solution to announce. Despite the unacceptance of your demise. I shall turn you into a spirit so that you can be able to utilize your potential by possessing anyone on Earth. Will that be satisfied you enough?"

"Thank you, Death. I appreciate your offer. But for billions of people in the living world. Whom should I start with?"

"You must possess one of the newborns born each day or night. Most importantly, anytime or in years; don't be afraid to call me if you're prepared to face your eternal life. Nothing will stop you from doing what you must accomplish. Unless it happens from your reconsideration that you might want to put down this odd offer I recommended. Then you have to hand me your flair, and I could give it to someone else who is worthy and brave of taking the vulnerability. There are no created restrictions, and conditions that might conflict with you afterward when you're doing this unusual decision. And for the record, I haven't done anything as much as this abnormal service you caused for the rest of my eons. It's kind of a little silly thing for me to realize, to be honest."

"I might be given different names by a birth giver, but my qualities as a prodigy would still stay in me. Whether my subject would be a boy or a girl, they'll be a gifted child like me. However, the silent plague of trauma and sadness from my collective unconsciousness—these children I'll possess will be broken as well, aside from being so intellectual. I could say myself I'm a pill with different side effects, in a nutshell."

"But are you willing to let any child feel your pain, and endure it internally as you do?"

"No. I avoid that to happen. And if that's the case, I must stay out of them as possible."

"But if you leave, how could you pursue your dreams?"

"Don't worry. I tolerate it. I know it already, so don't fret. Of course, I'll become their blessing by turning them into young prodigies. But, at the same time, I'll be a curse and interruption to their sanity. I'll be their muse who gives artistic gifts and directions to them. And I am, either, the resemblance or birth of a tortured artist. If I sense that there's something worse will happen to the children because of my flaws. I'm not afraid to leave. I would leave just for them to feel certain peace and happiness. No matter I utilize my flair very little."

"That's the most thoughtful act you have considered, Charlie. I will bring you back to Earth, and I'll wait for your latest response sooner about sending you to heaven."

About the Author

Michaella Erica was born in the Philippines on 15 September 2003, and she's studying Multimedia Arts at Systems Technology Institute (STI College). She joined CHWG (Coffee House Writers Group) for almost three years, where she can learn more about writing with help from other writers.

She started writing fantasy stories as a practice at the age of 13. And through multiple trials, she has found her voice belonged to tales that are darker, gothic, surreal, and connected to psychological and drug themes.

When discovering books that are experiential and thwart the traditional modes of writing. She is highly inspired to try out something uncommon and absurd in her craft. And become one of those literary artists who refuses to stay within the boundaries of traditional structures of writing, as well as standard genres and tropes, by pushing them in new ways.